INVASION

Wire Ones

by Laurence Staig
Illustrated by Stella Voce

LONGMAN

PROLOGUE

The Investigators of the Unexplained sat in two neat rows in front of the television set. Eleanor and Oliver Elmtree were in separate armchairs. The Otter twins, Simon and Matthew, sat together on the edge of Mr and Mrs Ronald and Virginia Elmtree's settee, perfectly mirroring one another's expressions and movements. They all wore deadly serious faces, as they were expecting important news from Astronomer Patrick Morris, Observer of the Heavens, host of *The Sky Tonight*.

At last, advertisements for a new chain of dry cleaners finished and the booming, earthy orchestral theme music for *The Sky Tonight* filled the room.

Eleanor and Oliver fidgeted in anticipation. The Otter twins merely crossed their legs in perfect unison, like a pair of symmetrical swimmers.

The large, bushy-eyed form of Patrick Morris filled the screen. His eyebrows seemed bushier than usual. His habitual frown was furrowed into a far more serious position.

"Exciting news. The mysterious asteroid, recently detected by astronomers, is due to come within the earth's orbit on April the 30th. We are still uncertain where it has come from, and about its makeup. However, we do know that it appears to be moving in a strange elliptical orbit, almost as if it was a powered vessel, like a space craft. Of course, we know that that is quite impossible. There is a possibility that the earth's gravity might pull the asteroid into our atmosphere, where it will break up into debris. This would fall to earth giving us a most amazing firework display! In fact, it could be the firework display of the century. So – keep watching the skies, and keep watching *The Sky Tonight*, for further updates."

The Otter twins turned to the Elmtrees. Together they nodded the nod that knew.

"Now then," continued Patrick Morris, "on to other matters. Things really do seem to be hotting up in Alpha Mercury, probably due to the influence of an emerging black hole!"

Eleanor slipped off her chair and switched the television off. The twin moon faces of the Otter twins were unified in expression and opinion.

"What do you think, Twigs?" Oliver asked his sister.

"What do you think?" asked Simon Otter.

"I suspect an alien invasion," said Eleanor, tossing her hair bunches back over her shoulders. "We must be aware."

CHAPTER 1

Eleanor Elmtree carefully unwrapped another blackcurrant and liquorice sweet, sighed, popped it into her mouth and with narrowed eyes scanned the skies again.

Where were they?

She stopped sucking on her sweet for a moment and stared at a suspicious-looking woolly cloud cluster. It was gathering its bulky form, like a swarm of dandelion seeds, away in the distance. For a moment it seemed to move in an unnatural way. Then it shimmered, just to the right of the Dale Health council flats.

"Mmm," said Eleanor to herself, pondering again. "No, too obvious: they'd never hide behind clouds, they know we're wise to that one."

She was certain that they were here already. Perhaps they had been here for years and had taken on human form. Or maybe animal? She thought about the asteroid that was approaching earth and wondered if there might be a connection.

For a moment, Eleanor considered her faithful dog, Sidney the beagle. Oliver, her younger brother, had put the idea into her head, and now it popped back again.

Sidney might not be quite what he seemed. Sidney the beagle could well be the captain of an alien star fleet, sent here ahead of the invasion to assess carefully our strengths and weaknesses, maybe even to grade us and send reports back to the fleet, just like Mr Paddock-Smith's reports that were sent home to her parents at the end of each term.

"No way," she decided, "not Sidney - he's far too stupid."

She crunched on a particularly hard bit of the sweet, and allowed the lovely liquorice taste to leak out on to her tongue. They were good sweets to chew when considering the Unexplained.

Then, Eleanor reconsidered, maybe the Invaders were clever. Perhaps Sidney was just *pretending* to be stupid. Just supposing that at night, when they had all gone to bed, Sidney switched on her dad's computer and, with a few swift paw movements across the keyboard, passed security codes and hacked his way into the Prime Minister's computer, the one that protected us from our enemies, the one which the government always denies having. Perhaps Sidney passed on all our secrets to the fleet, which was getting nearer, and nearer, and nearer with each hour. The asteroid!

Eleanor felt a dark empty space at the pit of her stomach.

"Sidney ... Maybe Sidney's an alien after all!"

She felt hot, flushed and nervous. She widened her eyes and searched the clouds with even greater intensity. Had that been a silver saucer-shaped object, which had passed through the dandelion cluster moments earlier? No. It had been a plane, an ordinary boring plane. It always was.

Eleanor sighed and swallowed the remains of her sweet. Being an Investigator of the Unknown, of the Unexplained, of the Paranormal, was such a responsibility. She pushed her large, red plastic-framed specs back up on to her nose, and shook her hair bunches back over her shoulders.

"One must always be on the lookout," she whispered to herself. "Remember the motto: *be aware.*"

She looked up into the skies again. The Unknown stared back at her, its vast empty unseeing eyes a promise of the unfolding of reason. For a moment the explanation of that which can never be explained seemed just within her reach.

Suddenly, something horrible, dark, wet and clinging flopped on to her face. Eleanor screamed!

CHAPTER 2

Eleanor pulled at the terrible fleshy thing that covered her face. Her worst fears sprang to mind. It was an alien, trying to take her over – it must be! As she opened her mouth to scream, the alien tried to climb over her tongue, lured by the wonderful smell of black currant and liquorice. It was well known that Zorgs of the planet Zorga loved liquorice.

Somebody called out at her, from behind.

"Stargazer! Stargazer!"

Eleanor's heart doubled its beat. She pulled at the thing, fearing it might be a 'face-hugger' which, Simon Otter had assured her, lived on the planet Arcturus.

Glancing down at her hands, she was mildly disappointed to find that she held an old grey flannel. In one corner, by a ragged hole, was the initial 'W'. For just a moment she felt very silly. Very silly indeed.

"Stargazing again, Twigs?" asked a thin-faced boy, with marmalade-coloured hair and freckles as large as five penny pieces.

"Take a hike, Blotch!" seethed Eleanor, trying to remain as unruffled and dignified as she could manage.

'Blotch' was Wilf Duffy, a friend of the Investigators. He hated the nickname. Wilf made a pretend pair of binoculars with his hands and studied the skies, standing with his feet wide apart.

"Over there, Twigs!" cried Wilf, as he twisted round and pranced about like a demented Arkadian demon. "There was a Martian scout ship and you missed it!"

"Get lost … " called a voice.

" … Blotch!" came another.

The command came out of nowhere, in stereo, from a pair of voices. They were almost perfectly matched, except one of the voices was ever so slightly lower than the other. Eleanor heard one voice come from the right, behind her, and the other from the left.

Like a pair of matching hi-fi speakers, the Otter twins, Simon and Matthew, glided into position on either side of Eleanor – twin moon faces, orbiting the scene.

Wilf lowered his imaginary binoculars and stared with disdain at the newly arrived sentinels.

"Take your disgusting rag … " began Matthew.

" … with you," completed Simon.

"Yes, take it with you now," confirmed the pair, speaking together this time.

Eleanor held out Wilf's flannel, and surveyed the item at arm's length, staring down her nose.

"I was only mucking about," said Wilf sheepishly.

Eleanor felt sorry for him. It wasn't like her to use unkind nicknames, but he did behave so stupidly at times. Wilf rummaged in his backpack for his swimming things and unwrapped a badly folded towel. A school exercise book tumbled out on to the pavement and into the edge of a puddle. Wilf groaned.

"Here," said Eleanor, still holding the flannel at a safe distance, as though it might contain a plague virus from a pirate space craft. She approached Wilf and picked up his book. Then she dropped the flannel on to the towel.

"I'd wring it out first before you put it in your bag," said Eleanor.

"And apologise … ," said Matthew in the snootiest tone he could muster.

"To Eleanor … Yes, apologise," repeated Simon. "Right now," he added, as an afterthought.

In the distance, they could hear the warning pips of Dale Heath Middle School. It was time to go. Simon peered ahead. Behind the railings, a flurry of busy figures jostled and hurried across the playground like urgent ants. The first day of the new term always went like clockwork. Mr Paddock-Smith, the head teacher, always ensured that the first assembly was a 'model' one so you had to be on time. Things went downhill from then on. However, there were bonuses back in the classroom. For example there were the marvellous art and crafts lessons to look forward to, and the wonderful Mr Polkinghorne who gave them.

As Eleanor helped Wilf put his things back into his bag, a bicycle passed close by. It missed them narrowly, but splashed the puddle on to Wilf's backpack.

"Hey!" cried Eleanor.

Wilf screwed up his face as he recognised the flaky red bicycle frame, and the gangly figure who rode it. A stupid grin appeared from over a grey-jacketed shoulder. The Otter twins stared back at the scissor-sharp features.

"Better get a move on, Investigators," sneered Charlie Watkins. "Don't want to be late *dooo weeeee?*"

Eleanor said nothing. Instead she watched Charlie wobble along on the bicycle, as if he was only just learning how to ride. There were those at school who realised the Investigators' mission, and those who simply didn't understand at all.

All of a sudden, the four children heard a crack from somewhere in the sky. It was like the crack of a whip, but much louder. *Much louder.*

Eleanor glanced upwards, searching for a jet plane or a similar flying machine. Perhaps it was Concorde, or maybe *something* better. But there was nothing to be seen.

"Look!" shouted Wilf, pointing in the direction of the industrial estate, beyond the school.

Eleanor twisted round, just in time to see a blue fork of

lightning shoot down from a dark wispy cloud, low on the horizon.

"Lightning!" said Wilf, "and it looks as if it's hit one of the warehouse units."

"That's not lightning," cried Eleanor. "That's an electrical charge, a mysterious unidentified electrical charge!"

She clapped her hands. Matthew thought to himself that lightning *was* an electrical charge.

They waited, expecting to see flames, but there were none. Then the strange cloud seemed to break into curling strands, which were caught up on the gathering breeze and whisked up and away, like a whirlwind of wispy streamers. The children watched in wonder.

"What was *that?*" asked Simon and Matthew.

"They will be amongst us very soon," declared Eleanor solemnly. "They may come in human form." She turned to the Otters. "Or not."

The moon faces of the Otters twitched nervously.

"Rubbish," said Wilf, "that's just lightning, bog ordinary lightning! It'll rain soon and … "

A cackle cut Wilf short.

Eleanor watched a long looming shadow crawl into her view from the right, sliding on to the pavement like a dark veil.

"Isn't it time you were all inside?" came a voice, low but firm, which hissed like a snake.

A black glove landed firmly on Eleanor's shoulder. It gripped her for a moment and then, almost as suddenly, changed into a friendly pat. Slowly she looked up.

Above her stood a tall figure in a long black cloak, dressed like an undertaker. A black beard covered most of his face, and narrow green eyes stared down at her from beneath a huge black fedora hat, with a golden band.

"Come, my little friends," said the man. "Come, my watchers of the skies. Come. It is late. I'm your new teacher this term. My name is Mr Kite. I can see that you appreciate the strange, the unusual. Let us get to lessons. I shall show you such wonders then, such wonders."

For just a second, Eleanor thought she saw a small fork of blue light dance in his black gloved hand. Something twisted and glowed. Then, with a sweeping gesture, like a magician's secret pass, he showed his palm to be empty.

"Come, come follow Mr Kite," he commanded.

The Otter twins gulped, one after the other.

CHAPTER 3

Eighth-year Einsteins shifted uneasily on their bench seats. Seventh-year Newtons craned their heads, to check out the far side of the hall. Sixth-year Pasteurs cupped their hands and whispered into one another's ears. The Otter twins kept turning their heads toward each other as though they were mechanical toys, sharing one another's anxieties.

Eleanor Elmtree, who was sitting behind the Otters, screwed up her nose and watched Mr Paddock-Smith through the far windows as he glided along the corridor which separated the hall from the classrooms. He floated like a will o' the wisp in search of a suitable tarn to haunt.

Repeatedly, he kept looking at his watch, and turned to gaze down the corridor. Then he would shake his head and be seen to mutter beneath his breath. Mr Paddock-Smith was a chemistry teacher by training, methodical and scientifically precise. Calling the school Houses after famous scientists had been his idea.

Back in the hall, a question was being whispered along the Einstein House line.

"Where, where is he?"

The acting deputy head teacher, who usually stood at the front of the first-day-back assembly until Mr Paddock-Smith had made his ceremonious entrance, was missing. Popular Mr Polkinghorne, with the special 'B' allowance to look after art and crafts at Dale Heath Middle School, was nowhere to be seen.

Mr Polkinghorne usually gave the signal for everyone to stand, with a gentle wave of his hand and a wide-eyed expression – like an urgent owl or, as Matthew Otter had once observed, like the Queen. Sometimes it was simply a gesture of an index finger. Sixth-year Pasteurs looked around once more. Who would give the signal? Who was going to prepare Mr Paddock-Smith's entrance?

Mrs Moriarty of Home Economics stared anxiously through the hall windows at Mr Paddock-Smith, who was now unable to hide his state of agitation. How could he possibly enter the hall at the start of a new term without being acknowledged? Besides, the bell needed to be tolled, twice: it was the custom. It was respect.

"Polky's … "

" … gone missing," completed Simon Otter.

"Paddock'll go … " continued Matthew Otter.

"Spare!" chipped in Boris Ming, a helpful classmate.

Eleanor Elmtree observed it all, in detail. Suddenly there was a noise in the corridor. Mrs Stathos, the school secretary, flew from the direction of the headteacher's office with a piece of notepaper in her hand. Her cotton dress billowed out, making her look more like a balloon man than the arranger of school buses and dispenser of sticky plasters, TCP disinfectant and aspirins. For a moment, Mr Paddock-Smith looked very put out. He shook his head, obviously in disapproval. Then he froze. He had seen something behind her.

Wilf pursed his lips. He had been put at the front for talking as he had walked into the hall, and he had the best view from where he stood.

The figure rose out of nowhere like an emerging genie, his arms wide, gesturing with his huge hands. He towered above Mrs Stathos and Mr Paddock-Smith.

Although he was without his distinctive hat this time, Eleanor recognised him immediately. It was the strange man who had been outside the school gates, and who had earlier announced that he was their new teacher. She watched as Mr Paddock-Smith took the note from Mrs Stathos, hurriedly read it and shot out his hand to Mr Kite, whose stick insect

arm was already extended in greeting. The three spent a moment or two in deep discussion, then Mr Kite entered the hall.

The Otter twins shot a glance at Mrs Moriarty who they heard take an intake of breath. "My word," she was heard to murmur, as Mr Kite stepped into the hall with a determined stride. He was an awesome figure.

Mr Kite surveyed the hall. There was absolute silence, as cold and as clear as winter crystal. One could almost hear Mr Paddock-Smith's plants grow as they stood to attention in a line on the little proscenium stage. Mr Kite's gaze held every child's as he stretched out his arms and seemed to grow like a giant bat unfolding its wings.

Eleanor was convinced that he was staring at her. But Matthew and Simon both experienced the same sensation. Wilf stepped back, lowered himself and tried to hide amongst the fifth-year Darwins. Even little Eric Needle thought he had been singled out by Mr Kite's special gaze.

Mr Kite's eyes, twinkling like a pair of silver orbs, flashed across the assembled children. As he pushed out his jet black, glossed beard, a grin grew within the dark thatch. A single curled finger reached out into the air. With a strange gesture that was not unlike, yet not quite the same, as Mr Polkinghorne's when he introduced assembly, Mr Kite gestured to the school to rise.

Somewhere in the corridor, the twin tones of a bell sounded, ringing eerily like the slow scratch of a train's wheels on rails. As though under the control of a hypnotist's spell, the school rose as one.

Ceremoniously, his piece of notepaper held out in front of him, Mr Paddock-Smith entered. Mr Kite seemed to fold back on to a chair, just in front of Miss Forester, the PE teacher.

Mr Paddock-Smith appeared oddly nervous. This was unusual. He was ordinarily a man in control: confident, assured.

"I ... I ... ," Mr Paddock-Smith began. "I have been handed a note. I am very sorry to say that Mr Polkinghorne has been taken ill whilst away on his holiday and is unable to be with us until later in the term. We ... we are fortunate to have been sent a replacement teacher from County Hall ... an arts and crafts specialist, just like Mr Polkinghorne."

Mr Paddock-Smith glanced over at Mr Kite and forced a smile. Mr Kite returned the acknowledgement with ease, and he flexed his arms as though stretching tired wings.

"Er ... Mr Kite. We'd like to welcome you to Dale Heath Middle School."

All eyes turned on Mr Kite now. He twisted on his chair and bowed. Now it was possible to see more of his appearance. He wore a black shirt, buttoned at the neck, his waistcoat was a paisley patterned silk, also buttoned at the front. His trousers were black, and baggy with numerous pleats like a Cossack's. They seemed to flap about him as if he might have spindles for legs.

Mr Kite's voice was low, but insistent.

"I will be taking over Mr Polkinghorne's mobiles project, the new project that he had been planning. I shall show you how to make mobiles so fantastic that they will capture and play with the songs of the stars."

He laughed. "Songs of the stars, I say."

"What mobiles project?" whispered Simon to Eleanor.

Eleanor whispered in return, "We must be aware."

Mr Kite flashed a glance of stone at Eleanor, as if he had heard every word she had said.

CHAPTER 4

The corridor which led to the arts and crafts department hustled and bustled with excitement. Usually, Mr Paddock-Smith's instructions were clearly and exactly obeyed. Corridor number 4 was known as 'the runway', the taxi area that allowed dismissed classes access to the delights of the rest of Dale Heath Middle School. The runway was to be kept clear at all times, except of course to allow a class to make its way – or taxi – to the next classroom. But today was different: classes ran into each other, there were murmurs in the air, mutterings on the breeze, rumour ran rife.

"Amazing! Wicked! Double wicked!!" declared Orville Dargan, from New York, whose parents worked on the nearby American air force base.

"What was double … "

"Wicked?" completed Simon Otter, whose geography book was in serious danger of being pushed up his right nostril.

"Ohhh, that guy, that guy!" exclaimed Orville, in a further surge of passionate expression. He rolled his eyes upwards, "Outa sight man, outa sight! I mean, what a show, what a show! Get down! Awesome, truly, truly awesome!"

Further down the corridor another group of kids, who were in Einstein House, were busy explaining to Seventh-year Pasteurs, that they had seen amaaaazing things. Amaaaazing.

"What's this all about, Otters?" asked Eleanor, who had already whipped out her notebook from her shoulder-bag.

For a moment both Otters seemed ready to reply, but Eleanor was on the mark and raised a warning eyebrow. Matthew swallowed his tongue and allowed his brother to take the lead.

"Hold it, Otters. Speak one at a time, not together, not now."

"OK, Twigs," said Simon, "It's Mr Kite, the new teacher. Well, he's really cool."

"Cool, cool nonsense!" snapped Eleanor. "Tell me in proper English. Remember, you're a member of the Investigators of the Unexplained. We need proper, commonsense English!"

Simon looked suitably sheepish.

"Mr Kite … "

" … has been making a great impression with his classes," interrupted Matthew perfectly. "It's all the talk amongst the Einsteins. He's been making wind chimes and mobiles with them, all out of wire. He's a wow."

"Mmm," replied Eleanor, "Be careful Investigators. Don't be taken in. Be careful, I don't think our Mr Kite is all the supply teacher that he seems."

Eleanor Elmtree nestled her head into the gap between the railings. She glanced at her 'Alien IV' watch and sniffed indignantly. It was way past the time for meeting Oliver Elmtree Junior from school. Oliver always stayed late for after-school activities, so that his older sister could collect him. However, never, never ever had she been kept waiting this long before.

Suddenly, from the far corner of the Dale Heath First School quadrant, she spied a flurry of small people. A round wired pair of spectacles caught the sun, much the same as her own, but these were clearly her younger brother's, and not the expensive designer plastic that made up her own frames.

"Oliver!" yelled Eleanor.

Oliver Elmtree pulled himself away from the cluster. The children were busy like bees around a honey pot. Most of them appeared to be holding some kind of stick in the air, on the end of which there seemed to hang a string of glittering objects. They sparkled as a breeze caused them to

twist and reflect the colours of a rainbow.

"Hurry up, you're late!" called Eleanor. "I wonder what they've got there?" She was torn between irritation and curiosity.

Like a parting wave, the group dispersed and the person who had been hidden within their midst was revealed. Eleanor swallowed hard and stood up straighter. Carefully she adjusted her own spectacles and narrowed her eyes once more. This time she glanced up to the sky, and she wasn't certain why.

A gaunt, scarecrow-like woman stood in front of the school. She wore dark glasses, and had long bible-black hair, sleek and glossed like a shiny wig. Her lips were full and dark. Eleanor found it difficult to make out the rest of her features in detail. Somehow, she looked like a shop mannequin.

Oliver ran ahead of his friends. He held a cane rod out in front of him at the end of which hung a collection of moon- and star-shaped objects that seemed to catch the light in an odd kind of way, as he trundled along.

"Look Eleanor, look!" he called excitedly. "We've a new teacher and she showed us things, such wonders she called them!"

Eleanor straightened her back. "*Such wonders?*" She had heard that before.

"Look! Wind chimes, magical wind chimes!" continued Oliver, dancing with glee. "Moon beams! She calls them star gates, jewellery of the gods!"

Eleanor held her younger brother firmly by the shoulder and gently shook him.

"Tell me, tell me now! Who is your new teacher?"

"Why, there she is, behind us. Miss Moonfleet is her name. Miss Perkins, our regular teacher, was taken ill on holiday!"

CHAPTER 5

Eleanor inspected Oliver's mobile very carefully. She kept glancing behind him as she examined the metal constructions which hung like the strange sets of earrings her mother sometimes wore. The black-haired lady waved at them for a moment, and then turned on her heels and vanished back inside the school.

Eleanor ran a finger along the nylon fishing thread which attached the objects to the cane rod. There was a pair of interlocking triangles intertwined in such a clever way as to make them seem like an impossible puzzle. There were wire moons: crescent shapes, with crook noses. There were question-mark shapes and exclamation marks. The most striking feature of all was that they had been made from a brilliant shining metal, more reflective than the chrome cowhorn-styled handlebars adorning the huge motor bike which Mr Otter had been restoring in his garage for years and years.

"What is it supposed to be?" asked Eleanor quietly, trying to appear casual, but betraying her concern by pushing her spectacles further back on to her nose. Oliver noticed the gesture.

"What's the matter, Twigs?" Oliver asked. "There's nothing wrong, is there? It was a great lesson, honest, I mean … "

"What is it, though?" continued Eleanor.

"Like I said, Twigs, it's a mobile wind chime!"

"A mobile … "

"Yeah, it's great, really neat. Miss Moonfleet says that we should hold it as high as we can when a good breeze gets up and it sings! Look I'll show you."

Oliver held the rod out in front of him, but there was no sign of any breeze. Around them, Oliver's fellow classmates were scampering away with similar versions of the mobile wind chime held in their hands.

"We can talk to the stars!" said little Mary Gentle as she passed by, running towards her mother.

"What did she say?" asked Eleanor.

Older brothers and sisters, and mums with prams and shopping, admired the new gadgets.

"Come on," said Eleanor, "let's cut through the Wedge. The Otters and I thought we saw lightning strike one of the units earlier."

'The Wedge' was the local nickname for the industrial estate. It had been built in the shape of a wedge, with units that were sited in clusters at the southern end of Dale Heath Road and which narrowed to just a few in the north. This industrial wedge divided the local housing estates, one of which was council, the other private.

"What d'you mean, lightning?" sniffed Oliver, waving his wind chime in front of him in a way that Eleanor found distracting. The shapes appeared to blur, and cross into one another so that if you watched them for long enough, you began to feel dizzy.

"It was just after I saw you into the playground," said Eleanor, "I was doing my sky watch, because I thought there were some odd cloud formations this morning."

"Any sightings, Twigs?" asked Oliver.

"No." She sucked through her teeth, in thought. "At least I didn't think there were any, but there was very little sign of bad weather – you know, the kind you usually get before you see a UFO. But right out of nowhere there was this flash. I just want to see, that's all."

For a while Eleanor went quiet, striding out with determination, her bunches swinging clumsily at the sides of her head. They passed rows of empty units. TO RENT signs loomed in the windows, written in large red letters. Their father called the place 'a white elephant'. Businesses had been expected to boom there, but very few units had been rented out.

Mr Bennet waved at Eleanor and Oliver from the window as they passed the Futon Factory. It had only recently opened, and Eleanor knew from what her father had told her that he was already having problems ensuring that the business would survive.

Eleanor decided to speak about Mr Kite. "We've got a new teacher too, Oliver," she said at last.

"Really?" replied Oliver with mild interest, still fingering one of the moon-shaped objects attached to his rod.

"Look, do put that thing away. Pay attention. Remember, if you're to be one of our team, you must be aware."

"Sorry, Twigs," said Oliver. "Be aware," he repeated to himself.

"Mr Polkinghorne was taken ill during the hols. We've got this strange-looking teacher called Mr Kite. He's only temporary, but he's already the talk of the school. I'm not sure about him. We have art tomorrow. It sounds as if he's got a lot in common with your Miss Moonfleet."

"Miss Moonfleet's great. She talks funny though. Not properly, like you do when you ask someone something or … "

"What *do* you mean?" asked Eleanor, "'talks funny'?"

"Yeah, you know. I mean, instead of saying 'Now listen class, today we're going to learn how to make wind chimes, or mobiles', she says 'Let's be … ' what was it now, 'makers of ways', er, 'Let's get keys to explore the universe', something like that."

"Explore the universe?" repeated Eleanor, thoughtfully. "She said that to your lot – the class that has trouble understanding 'Walk on the left hand side of the corridor' and 'Keep your lockers locked'?"

Oliver nodded.

Eleanor went into thoughtful mode again, pressed her index finger against her nose and wandered ahead of Oliver.

"Is the unit this way?" asked Oliver, "Sidney used to like to walk round here, but not anymore. Dad said he growls and won't move when he takes him down this road."

"It was in this direction, but I don't know which unit got hit, if it was hit at all. I really just wanted to have a look in case … you know, report to the Otters and … "

"Twigs, look out!" Oliver's warning came just in time.

A van came suddenly out of nowhere and shot round the corner, just where Eleanor was about to step off the pavement. Eleanor gasped, and stumbled backwards.

"What was that?" cried Oliver.

"I don't know!" snapped Eleanor. "Where did it come from? I'm darn well going to find out!"

With that, she hurried around the corner and peered down the road, searching for any sign of the van. She couldn't see any vehicle at first, then Oliver caught up with her and pointed down the long empty rows of units.

"Look!"

Eleanor screwed her eyes up tight. She couldn't see anything. "What are you on about?"

"There," said Oliver. "No wonder it came as a surprise – it's almost invisible. It's just like a mirror."

Eleanor squinted again. The light was changing colour, producing a blue tinge, which bled into everything around them like an ink blot. Then she saw the van at the bottom of the road: it was highly polished with a mirror finish, almost like chrome.

"I've never seen a van like that before," said Oliver.

"And it almost ran me over!" said Eleanor angrily. "This is the direction we want to go, so come on!"

Oliver wrapped the strings of his mobile around the rod, and pushed it into his shoulderbag. Together they marched towards the far cluster of units. As they passed them Oliver noticed that some had been vandalised with graffiti. Strange patterns had been daubed on a few – designs that he had never seen before. Most of the graffiti on the estates was the usual boring and unimaginative stuff such as 'Simon Otter's a wally'. These patterns were something else: almost an alien language.

Oliver stopped for a moment. The units here had not been let since the time they were built. They were also the farthest out of town.

"Come on!" snapped Eleanor. "We have work to do."

Oliver peered at an unusual trio of interlocking triangles. As they neared the van, Eleanor put out her hand for Oliver to slow down. Ahead of them they saw that the huge doors of Unit Nine were half open. Two figures were carrying a large cardboard carton towards the doors. Suddenly a sour face with a pair of steely eyes appeared from behind the door. From where Eleanor and Oliver were standing, it was just possible to overhear their conversation.

"Hurry up, we need another rail!" hissed the sour-faced man.

The other two who were carrying the box, moved with slow angular movements, as though they might have rusty hinges in their joints. One of them suddenly turned round and glared at Eleanor. For a moment she thought he might be wearing a mask over his face.

"Clear off! Now!" cried the sour-faced man.

"You nearly ran my sister over," began Oliver. "You really should be more … "

"NOW!" repeated the man.

Suddenly, Eleanor had one of her feelings – the kind of feeling that only a truly experienced Investigator of the Unexplained can have; it was a moment of insight, of knowing the truth of all things. Eleanor Elmtree knew that they had to get out of there.

"Come on! Let's go!" she said, and she grabbed Oliver by the hand.

"Why? They should be more careful!"

Eleanor pulled him behind her.

Further along the east road, they stopped and turned to look back. They now had a view of the northern side of the unit.

"Look," said Oliver, a puzzled expression crossing his face.

Eleanor saw it too. She thought that it might be a giant shadow, but it wasn't.

"What's that?" asked Oliver.

A black sooty mark stretched up towards the roof. It was twisted at one end, making the shape of a tornado.

"It's a burn," said Eleanor solemnly. "It was either caused by a fire, or it was made by lightning. Darn it, that was the unit that was hit by that electrical charge! I wonder what their business is?"

Above them, just as before, the clouds were gathering again, rolling along the roof of the sky as though with minds of their own. The blue-edged light threw a crystal tinge across the ground, making their shadows darker and sharper than ever.

CHAPTER 6

As usual the Elmtree household was in turmoil when Oliver and Eleanor reached home. Their father had arrived back earlier than expected and was stretched out like a long plank on Sidney the beagle's favourite chair. He held his newspaper out in front of him, but he wasn't really reading it. He was hiding from their mother.

"She knows it's difficult in the summer!" cried Mrs Elmtree. "Sometimes I think she does it on purpose. Aunt Eloise is always welcome, you know that, but it's usually Christmas time when she visits!"

"Yes, Virginia dear, absolutely," came a response from behind the newspaper.

Sidney made a small whimpering noise and glanced upwards. His deep and sad brown eyes showed that he wished that Mr Elmtree would hurry up and get out of his chair.

"Hi, mum! Hi, dad!" called Eleanor from the hallway, where she and Oliver had been waiting, trying to decide on the right moment to make an entrance.

There was no reply.

"I mean, where would we put her? I'm going to be late for this appointment, you know!"

Mrs Elmtree rushed across the room, stopping for a moment to inspect her newly-cleaned pink dress, which hung like a limp skin from a hook at the back of the lounge door.

"Oh no, they haven't managed to get that stain out! Serves me right for trying out that new cleaners. What time is it?"

"Yes, dear," said Mr Elmtree, from the safety of his chair.

Sidney the beagle made a gurgling noise. Elearnor put her head round the door and glanced at the computer which sat in the corner of the room. Then she looked down at Sidney again, and decided that one of her earlier theories about him was probably a non-starter.

"Hi, mum! Hi, dad!" chirped Oliver.

"Look, look at this thing they've returned my dress on!" said Mrs Elmtree, popping her spectacles on to her nose. She pierced the plastic polythene cover and ran her finger over the wire hanger.

"No wonder it doesn't hang right!"

"Yes, dear," said Mr Elmtree, this time moving the newspaper to one side and peering at the two children who stood at the far end of the room.

Sidney also looked up and managed to make his tail twitch, in some kind of acknowledgement.

"Hi, kids," said Mr Elmtree, with a nod.

"You're late," said Mrs Elmtree in a matter-of-fact voice as she stepped back, to look at her dress once again.

"We came home through the Wedge," said Eleanor. "There are strange things going on there."

"Darlings, in your world there are ALWAYS strange things going on." She threw a purpose-made smile at them both, then stepped back and put her hands on the backs of both of their heads, pulling their faces into her. This was Mrs

Elmtree's standard quick embrace.

"My babies!" she said.

Oliver's glasses were pushed up into his face as he saw Eleanor's look of disapproval.

"I've got an important appointment with two clients at the estate in just over half an hour! I'm hoping to sell them a special insurance policy that will pay the bills this month. Someone has to make a success out of selling insurance!"

She glared at her husband. Eleanor's father also sold insurance, but he had not been having much luck with his batch of clients.

"I think something very odd *is* going on at the estate," said Eleanor, more firmly this time. "We saw boxes being moved into a new unit."

"Good!" replied Mrs Elmtree, "I had heard there were new people moving in. New business, nothing strange at all!"

"There's something strange all right," chipped in Mr Elmtree, finally putting his newspaper to one side and beginning to feel as if he was being got at. "Hardly any of those units are open and doing business, and those that did manage to have a go had to close. Nobody's making any money!"

Eleanor knew he was about to become really riled.

"Huh – always look on the bad side. I have to get another dress," said Mrs Elmtree as she swept out of the room and up the stairs.

Mr Elmtree looked very sorry for himself.

"Did our magazine come?" asked Eleanor, deciding to change the subject.

"What magazine?" He paused, pulling himself out of the chair and moving across to the table, where a pile of old newspapers were stacked ready to go out to the bins.

"Sorry, Twigs," he sighed, "I nearly threw it out."

Oliver snorted and pulled a glossy magazine out of his father's hands.

"It's all rubbish you know," said Mr Elmtree. "What's it called again?"

"World Mysteries: *The Unexplained*," announced Eleanor, with a note of pride in her voice, "and it is *not* rubbish. One never knows. One must be aware!"

"Hey," said Oliver, greedily turning the pages as if he had found a treasure map. "It's a special issue about parallel universes!"

"What in heaven's name is a parallel universe?" asked Mr Elmtree, raising his eyes to the ceiling.

"EVERYONE knows what a parallel universe is, Dad!" Oliver looked disgusted.

Mr Elmtree was about to sit back in the armchair when he heard a faint growl. Sidney the beagle had crept back into his chair.

"Sidney!" he yelled.

"Take no notice of Dad," said Eleanor, "he wouldn't know a parallel universe if he fell into one."

"It's another universe that is invisible, but runs alongside our own," said Oliver carefully. "It's an opposite. If it met its own image it would vanish! Positive and negative equals nothing! Simple mathematics."

"You're losing Dad," warned Eleanor.

Suddenly, from upstairs there came the most enormous scream. It echoed out in the hallway, and caused Sidney to sit bolt upright, something very unusual for a lazy beagle.

"Virginia!" cried Mr Elmtree.

"Help me!" came the reply.

Eleanor shot ahead of her father, followed by Oliver. Mr Elmtree came last, trying to squeeze past his two children. Oliver was the first on the scene. He pushed open his parents' bedroom door and gawped at what he saw. Eleanor pushed past him and stood over her mother, who was lying flat out on the huge double bed. For a moment she didn't know quite what to say, then her father's head appeared round the door and he simply burst into laughter.

"It's not funny!" protested Mrs Elmtree. "It was odd, I was reaching for my summer dress and suddenly – well, they all rushed out at me!"

"Rushed out at you!" laughed Mr Elmtree. "Oh, sure – alive were they?"

Mrs Elmtree was spread-eagled, her arms and legs outstretched, with piles of dresses and a tower of metal coat hangers lying on top of her. In front of her, the sliding doors of the wardrobe were still open, the garments jumbled into a mess.

Oliver looked up at his father, who was now almost doubled up with laughter, and he began to laugh too.

"I just reached in for my cotton summer dress, the cinnamon coloured one, that was all, and suddenly they all rustled, and there was this odd blue light, I mean … "

"What kind of light?" asked Eleanor seriously, picking her way through the remaining hangers, which were tangled in chains and hung like circus trapezes from the rail.

"I don't know! Look, get these things off me!"

Eleanor looked deeper into the wardrobe. From the corners something seemed to glow with a sinister light. She examined the hangers. They did not seem like the usual kind. They shone and sparkled like chrome.

They suddenly heard a howl from downstairs.

"Sidney?" asked Oliver suddenly.

Eleanor rushed downstairs, just in time to see the beagle trying vainly to dig a hole in his chair. He was whimpering, and clearly upset by something.

"Sidney!" said Eleanor. "What is it? What's the problem?"

For just a second, she thought she saw Sidney raise his eyes to the bedroom above, as though trying to tell them something. Eleanor believed she knew what it was.

CHAPTER 7

Mr Paddock-Smith paraded in front of the assembled school, hands firmly held behind his back. He alternately stared at the ceiling and then at the hall floor, making quite, quite certain that at no point did he turn to face any of the children.

The Otter twins held their breath, together.

Oliver Elmtree watched his prowl in fascinated silence, while Eleanor kept one watchful eye on Mr Kite, who seemed to have moved to the rear of the hall rather than sit along the side aisle with the rest of the teachers.

"Respect!" announced Mr Paddock-Smith at long last, maintaining his glance between heaven and earth. "That is what we are talking about here. Respect and pride. Pride in one's self and respect for one's classmates and their rights."

He suddenly turned to the school and glared as he pointed upwards with a single digit.

"Respect!"

The Otter twins nudged one another. From the side aisle stepped a solemn-looking Miss Merrydew in charge of drama. She moved towards the front.

"Miss Merrydew," said Mr Paddock-Smith, gesturing that she should take his position.

Miss Merrydew began.

"A lot of hard-working people spent many hours after school at the end of last term tidying the drama cupboard, making certain that all of the costumes were in the right places and in the correct order of size. A LOT of hard-working people."

"Are you listening!?" raged Mr Paddock-Smith. "You, Joy Edwards, see me after!"

"Now," continued Miss Merrydew, "somebody has been into the drama cupboard and totally destroyed our system! Glynis Duckworth, the drama props monitor, spent several lunch and break times clearing up the cupboard. Where there was once an orderly rack of comic costumes, there is now a heap of rags. Where we once had a dress rail of medieval costumes – jesters' outfits, ladies-in-waiting frocks, gentlemen's courtier apparel – there is now an entire chain of knotted garments."

"Are you listening?" interjected Mr Paddock-Smith. "Are you? Respect! Now, who is going to own up? Who is going to confess to this gross act?"

If someone had had a pin to drop, then it would have been heard there and then. The silence was as complete as could be found in the desert regions of the planet Nostromos. (According to Simon Otter it could be very quiet indeed there.) Oliver felt guilty, although he had done nothing. Orville Dargan was tempted to step out to the front, confess, and allow himself to be searched, like in the cop movies, although he was innocent too. Mr Paddock-Smith could have that effect on you.

Eleanor turned her head ever so slightly, to search out Mr Kite. He had lowered his head. He appeared to have half-closed his eyes, but their lizard glint remained. She was certain that he was watching, and waiting.

"Be aware," Eleanor reminded herself.

The big silence continued. The Otter twins twitched, alternately, then together.

"Very well," announced Mr Paddock-Smith at length. "I shall show you the kind of mindless vandalism we are talking about."

Miss Merrydew, her own head now bowed like that of an altar boy, walked to the far side of the hall to the drama cupboard. She opened the door and went in.

For several moments the sound of fumbling and the moving of objects could be heard. Then she finally appeared with one of the princess costumes. Eleanor immediately recognised it as the one that had been used in the pantomime last year. Miss Merrydew trailed the costume out from the cupboard, then held it up for all to see.

There was a gasp. The beautiful princess costume was torn to ribbons. The teachers, who sat in rows in the gangways, averted their eyes from the terrible sight.

But Eleanor Elmtree did not.

Oh no.

Eleanor Elmtree made a mental note of the hanger that the costume was hung upon. It was a bright chrome colour, with a brightness which was somehow far too bright. Just for a second, Matthew Otter thought that he saw a blue light throb from within the darkness of the drama cupboard. Surely something was lurking in there?

CHAPTER 8

Eleanor decided that she couldn't just hang around at the bottom of the Newtons' House corridor any longer. For some reason there was a nagging, niggling doubt, which wriggled around inside her: a feeling that all was not well in the art and crafts department.

Why was there no more information about Mr Polkinghorne? What did the message mean, 'taken ill'?

She had overheard the school secretary talking to one of the dinner ladies. This new teacher, Mr Kite, had shown up unannounced with just a postcard from County Hall with the school's address on it. Mr Paddock-Smith had brushed aside any suggestion that they should check with the staffing unit. "Of course he's odd. He's a supply teacher," had been his response. "Sloppy administration," Mrs Stathos had called it and then shut up when she saw Eleanor.

Most of Eleanor's class had already marched obediently into the art room. One or two latecomers, such as Eric Froggat (who was on report), wrestled with the door handle and then disappeared within the room. Eleanor heard the seductive voice of Mr Kite, as the door closed.

"Dooo come in, such wonders to show you." It was like syrup. The voice sent a shiver down Eleanor's back, making the tiny hairs on the back of her neck bristle.

She gulped. Pushing her spectacles more firmly on to the bridge of her nose, she advanced down to the end room.

"Oh Eleanor, dooo come in," said the voice from within the room, just as Eleanor reached out to turn the handle.

She was in.

"I'm sorry, sir," said Eleanor. "I was delayed by Miss Kember on my way here."

"How does he know my name?" Eleanor wondered.

"Sit down, make yourself comfortable," said Mr Kite.

He no longer wore his huge hat. His black hair was bunched up at the back, and held in place with a silver pin. She noticed that he was wearing gloves, black and sleek, as though they had been sprayed on to his hands. The perfect slender shape of his fingers flexed like the legs of a huge tarantula spider. His eyes were as bright as ever, brighter than blades.

Eleanor found it difficult to turn away from his gaze. But when she did, she saw that the rest of her class were all sitting on chairs arranged in rows in the shape of a crescent. All eyes were on Mr Kite. Even the Otter twins, who sat together at the front, were transfixed by Mr Kite's presence.

This was unusual. Seventh-year Einsteins Beta did not behave this well when a supply teacher came to visit. Although they were not devils, they were certainly not angels, and 'triers-on' such as Roger Stone (or 'Pebble' as he was known), usually tried out some scheme or caper.

Eleanor quietly made her way to the front. Matthew Otter nudged his brother who shifted his chair over, to allow another chair to be placed in between them. She sat down.

"Now," said Mr Kite, at last. "Let us begin."

A huge white sheet had been placed over a table. It was the big wooden table, usually used to display their pots when the class were working with clay. Eleanor could see various forms and shapes beneath the sheet, which dipped and rose in pinnacles and hills.

"*I wonder what's underneath,*" thought Eleanor.

Like a chef presenting a special secret banquet, Mr Kite made a circular motion, almost a flourish, with his hand and pulled away the sheet. There was a cluster of geometrical shapes on the table – star-shaped constructions, pyramids, orbs with circles within circles, all seemingly impossible shapes, and all astonishingly beautiful like giant snow crystals.

There was absolute silence in the room. Then one of the triangular shapes on the table twisted on one of its points and threw beams of light across the faces of the children. It was like a special light show.

There was a sharp intake of breath, as though a huge vacuum cleaner had descended above their heads. The leaves of paper in the pupils' folders lifted with the suction.

The Otter twins turned their heads and stared at one another across Eleanor. Eleanor nudged both of them with her elbows.

"Now," began Mr Kite, once more. "Please meet my collection of space jewellery, but given life, given powers beyond your wildest dreams. Such wonders, my little ones, such wonders. Let your special teacher show you how!"

Mr Kite signalled with a raised eyebrow to Berenice Basset to pull down the main blind which stretched along the work bench on the far wall. Mr Kite nodded at Ernie Kops, who obligingly twisted the Venetian blind cord plunging the art and crafts room into darkness.

A blue spotlight unexpectedly appeared on the table. At first it landed on one of the orbs, then it widened to a neighbouring sphere which started to spin of its own accord. It twisted round the other shapes, floating as though part of a magician's trick.

Mr Kite spoke. "Such fabulous, amazing treats!"

He clicked his fingers and allowed his hands to pass above the shapes, as though exerting a strange magical spell on the objects below.

"Look ... " whispered Simon Otter.

" ... at that," completed Matthew Otter.

One of the pyramidical shapes twisted up on one end and spun like a ballerina, faster and faster.

Another sphere danced into the air and then was joined by another which nudged it like a billiard ball. Together they made a sweep across the front edge of the table.

"Be amazed," hissed Mr Kite, almost beneath his breath.

"Mr Kite is very clever," said Glynis Duckworth, in a very matter-of-fact manner. "You can hardly see how he's making these objects move."

Glynis twitched her nose.

"In fact, I'm not sure that I can see at all how they work."

"Shut it, Quackers," said Wayne Lovell, rudely.

"What are they, sir?" asked Glynis.

"Space jewellery, I told you. Put them on the ends of special canes and you have wind chimes, mobiles that will talk to the universe."

Suddenly, Ernie Kops, who had been fiddling with the blind with more exuberance than was necessary, twisted the rod that operated the shutters and unexpectedly let in more light.

A shaft of sunlight suddenly hit the table.

Only Eleanor Elmtree and the Otter twins noticed.

"Truly weird," whispered Eleanor. "Mr Kite's hands are in his pockets now. How can he be operating those objects? How can they move?"

Simon turned and looked at her with that look, the look which only Investigators of the Paranormal KNEW.

There were strange forces at work here.

Just then Glynis Duckworth shot her hand up. She had remembered something important.

"Permission to go to the drama cupboard, sir. I've just remembered that Miss Merrydew wants me to take the dressing mirror there for her."

"Mirror?" asked Mr Kite, suddenly becoming strangely agitated.

"Yes, sir!" said Wilf Duffy, helpfully. "Mr Polkinghorne used to keep it at the back here. Drama often borrowed it!"

Before Mr Kite could say another word Wilf had bounded out of his chair to the back of the classroom and had opened the art provisions cupboard. He disappeared inside and reappeared carrying a full-length mirror, which was far too big for him to carry.

"Miss said I'm to take it," whined Glynis at Wilf.

"I've got it now, though!"

"Miss said … "

"OK," shrugged Wilf, "just helping."

Wilf leant the mirror against the wall. Suddenly a shriek rang out. Eleanor switched her view from Wilf and the mirror to the front of the class. Mr Kite had thrown up his hands in horror and was hurrying to shield his models from the reflection of the glass.

"Turn it to the wall! Quickly! Do as I say! They must not reflect!"

The class went silent. Mr Kite picked up a vase and threw it at the mirror, which smashed into dozens of pieces.

"Why on earth did he do that?" whispered Simon.

CHAPTER 9

"They've definitely changed the coat hangers," said Matthew Otter, reading from his spiral-bound notebook.

"I've asked around," interrupted Simon Otter.

"We both have," added Matthew. "Miss Merrydew … "

" … claims that at the end of last term the costumes had all been hung on the usual mixture of old coat hangers."

"Yeah," agreed Matthew.

"And it was Glynis that changed all the hangers?" asked Eleanor, making notes in her own spiral-bound reporter's notebook.

"You know what a goody-goody she is," sniffed Simon.

"Let me get this straight then. She says that she found this box of hangers?"

"That's right," said Simon. "She said that she liked them, thought they looked pretty, and that it would be a good idea to have all the coat hangers the same."

"She tidied the cupboard at the end of last term, but came in during the holidays to return a costume she had borrowed. The hangers were in a box at the back of the school, next to the bins. That's … "

" … when she swopped them over," finished Simon.

A sudden explosion almost caused the three Investigators to jump out of their skins. They looked up. Mr Paddock-Smith was reversing his old Morris Minor car, his pride and joy, through the school gates. A billow of black sooty smoke poured from the exhaust pipe.

"It's only Paddock's banger," said Matthew.

Eleanor peered into the distance. For some reason she glanced up at the skies. The clouds rolled and tumbled, nature was on the edge. For a moment everything about her seemed to freeze into one of those *moments in time*.

"Be aware," she said.

Eleanor watched as her classmates from the art and crafts group poured out of the west corridor exit. Several of them had completed the mobiles which they had been making in Mr Kite's lesson. They had been easy to make using wire frames. Eleanor and the Otters had been very slow in putting together their shapes. Something deep inside worried them. (Investigators of the Unexplained could have this kind of feeling about things sometimes. Eleanor called it a 'Psychic Hunch'.) Of the incident with the mirror, nothing had been said.

Mr Kite had told them all that the important step was to 'breathe life' into their mobiles, to make them live. "They need the light of the stars," he had said.

Simon wandered down towards the staff car-park and stopped short at the huge railings. Mr Paddock-Smith had got out of his car and was peering down the exhaust, scratching his head at the same time.

Eleanor suddenly remembered her brother Oliver. Today's meeting was important. They needed to catch up on what had been happening in Miss Moonfleet's classes.

The First School was close by. As they made their way down the path which linked the two schools, Eleanor became puzzled at the multi-coloured orbs that seemed to float towards her from the distance.

"Aliens!" declared Simon, rather prematurely.

"Soap bubbles," insisted his brother, with some authority.

Behind the school gates Eleanor could see groups of children dipping huge wire-framed hoops into red plastic buckets. They then held the hoops in the air and smiled as a breeze billowed into the circle, producing huge kaleidoscopic bubbles.

At the front of the crowd, a small boy was spinning like a whirling top, allowing clusters of bubbles to race one after the other, through his hoop. It was Oliver Elmtree.

"Look!" cried Oliver. "Soapy dreams, other worlds!"

"Soapy what?" said Eleanor.

"Miss Moonfleet helped us make them!" called another child behind Oliver. He swept his frame through the air as though it were a magician's wand. A pyramid of colour tumbled above their heads floating higher and higher.

From somewhere behind them, a familiar-sounding explosion echoed. Along the road which ran beside the green came Mr Paddock-Smith in his car again. This time, the car halted abruptly with a final bang. A cloud of soot billowed up from somewhere beneath the rear. The children heard a huge gasp, like an enormous wheeze, as steam escaped from either side of the bonnet.

Mr Paddock-Smith lowered his head into his hands and for a moment he simply sat there, uncertain what to do.

"That car's always going wrong," said Matthew.

"Never works properly," Simon chipped in.

"Look at my bubbles!" cried Oliver with glee, ignoring the commotion across the green.

But Eleanor was far more interested in Mr Paddock-Smith. He had now got out of the car and unlatched the bonnet and was furiously waving away the steam which billowed upwards into his face. The steam cleared quickly. Mr Paddock-Smith slowly and cautiously leant forward and peered into the engine housing.

His cry froze the Otters' blood.

Eleanor watched as Mr Paddock-Smith threw his hands up and staggered backwards.

"What is it?" cried the Otter twins.

Eleanor Elmtree turned to her fellow Investigators of the Unexplained and signalled for them to follow her. Within moments she had crossed the green to Mr Paddock-Smith, who stood staring at his car. He looked like a zombie from the planet Zardoz. His face had turned the colour of self-raising flour.

At first Eleanor thought that the engine had been covered with a silver fishing net of some kind. The Otters stood on either side of the car. Simon was looking at the engine from all angles, undecided exactly what it was that he should be looking for.

Oliver placed his hoop on the grass, glanced at the engine, and dared to say what the others were afraid of saying.

"The engine's all covered in wire! Why's that?"

Eleanor looked closer. A web of glistening chrome wire was tangled around all of the engine parts. The carburettor was knotted with loops and strands of the stuff, the radiator had been pierced with lengths of it and the fan belt had been tied up with a neat silver bow.

"Where did this come from, Mr Paddock-Smith?" asked Eleanor, throwing a serious glance at the headteacher.

"I ... I ... I don't know!"

"You didn't put any of this wire in there?" said Eleanor.

"No! Of course not! I only ... "

Mr Paddock-Smith fell silent. He went behind the car and opened the boot. For a second or two, the sun gleamed on the edge of a gleaming coat hanger, which he produced from a plastic carrier bag.

"My radiator hose was loose, so I made a temporary clip to fasten it. I used this wire coat hanger."

Eleanor took the hanger from Mr Paddock-Smith. He had cut out a section of it to make the clip. Slowly, she walked to the front of the car and examined the radiator hose. It matched. But it also matched the rest of the wire which seemed to have grown like some kind of wild Vesuvian spaghetti.

"I found the hanger in a box next to the drama cupboard," said Mr Paddock-Smith sheepishly. "I thought it was rubbish, to be thrown out."

The Otters exchanged glances.

Suddenly, Oliver ran over to the patch of grass where he had left his bubble hoop frame. He picked it up and looked at it closely.

Eleanor crossed over to where he stood and held the coat hanger beside it. It, too, was a perfect match.

She looked up at the sky.

"Be aware," she whispered.

"Look, there's Mr Kite!" shouted Simon, pointing at the First School entrance.

Eleanor's eyes followed the direction of his finger. A tall, slender figure stood in the entrance to the school.

"No," said Oliver, "that's Miss Moonfleet, *our* new teacher!"

Eleanor blinked. Shimmering, soapy bubbles of colour crossed in front of her, blown by a sudden upturn in the breeze. A blue glow seemed to reflect off everything around them. The image of Miss Moonfleet rippled as though it was a mirage in an Arkadian desert.

Then she grinned with a death's head grin.

CHAPTER 10

The mobile, which hung from the end of the rod, shuddered gently, like winter icicles on brittle branches. Eleanor prodded one of the chrome spheres with her finger then she turned an interlocking group of triangles, which tinkled and spun. Somehow, they did seem to have a life of their own, moving in a certain way, making tiny melodies that almost sounded as though they were a kind of fairy morse code. Eleanor murmured and pursed her lips. She and Oliver were having an emergency meeting of the Directors of the Investigators of the Unexplained in his bedroom, before tea.

"We've been making lots," said Oliver. "She's a weird teacher, but all of the lessons have been really interesting, and everyone looks forward to art lessons now. She said that the metal is special, that it can pick up radio waves."

"And what else?" asked Eleanor, moving her spectacles down towards the edge of her nose and looking over the edge.

"We make jewellery too. She seems to like us to use sharp-edged shapes."

"Sharp-edged shapes?" asked Eleanor.

"Yeah, you know: squares and triangles and things. Insists we measure them very precisely as if it was important."

"You mean geometrical shapes. We do that too with Mr Kite."

Oliver nodded, believing that Eleanor had probably used the right word.

"And what about those bubbles?"

"That was another thing. She said that we would make planets, shapes that came from another world. She was only making it all up to make it sound more interesting. But she did make a special frame in one of the lessons, a really peculiar-shaped thing that produced an enormous bubble. There seemed to be things inside, but it was only the reflection of the light on the soap."

"And I suppose the wire is ... ?"

Oliver nodded.

"Coat hangers," he said.

All of a sudden the bedroom door opened and a furry bundle trundled into the room, tail wagging. Sidney the beagle stopped for a moment and looked up at the mobile suspiciously, then he growled.

"See that?" said Eleanor, "I've noticed it before, when you first brought it home. Dogs know. They're psychic; they have special powers and know when something's not right."

She turned to her brother and placed her hand on his shoulder.

"Something's not right, now."

Sidney the beagle gave an approving growl.

From outside the room they heard the clump of their mother's feet as she passed the door.

"No room. As I live and breathe I can't go on: we need a bigger wardrobe!" she shouted. There was a note of desperation in her voice.

Eleanor motioned to Oliver to follow her.

In the hallway, Mrs Elmtree was ferrying a pile of her clothes from one room to the other.

"I'd swear my clothes must be expanding or that wardrobe must be shrinking. It's becoming a real chore just to hang up a blouse in there. Every time I open the cupboards something flies out at me. It's almost as though I was being attacked!"

Sidney raised an eyebrow, and lowered his tail.

She turned and saw the children, paused and disappeared into the spare bedroom.

"Your film is on soon," she called. "You asked me to remind you."

Oliver frowned and looked over at Eleanor. Her face suddenly glowed.

"I'd forgotten all about it!"

"What's that, Twigs?" asked Oliver.

"The SF film, the oldie in the Movie Classics slot! *The Thing From Another World!*"

"Utter nonsense," called their mother from the bedroom. They heard the sound of metal against metal.

"These damn coat hangers!"

Eleanor peered round the door. Sidney growled. Mrs Elmtree was wrestling with a pair of interlocking hangers.

"Try to untangle these, there's a dear," Mrs Elmtree handed the hangers to Eleanor. Oliver looked over her shoulder.

"Silver hangers," said Oliver knowingly.

"Yes, pretty isn't it, that strange colour? I didn't like them at first. I don't know where I got all these from, though. My wardrobe seems to be full of them now. I think they come from that new shop. I've got to call over at Mrs Johnson's - she collected my dry cleaning."

"Where do wire coat hangers usually come from?" asked Oliver.

Mrs Elmtree sighed.

"Don't you usually get given them back with your dry cleaning?" asked Eleanor.

"Well, yes. I mean, you don't buy them. They - well, they kind of grow. You kind of end up with them after a while."

Eleanor murmured.

"*The Thing's* coming on!" came a call from downstairs. It was their father. "You asked us to … "

"I know, Dad," replied Eleanor

"Go and watch it," said Mrs Elmtree. "I need to get going. I've been trying to call on that new company that's moved into the Wedge. If I don't sell some insurance soon we'll be in deep water!"

"New company?" asked Eleanor.

"Yep. Looks like they may need a really good policy. Seems as though they keep getting hit by lightning."

Eleanor said nothing.

CHAPTER 11

No matter what the Investigators of the Unexplained were investigating, a science-fiction movie was a science-fiction movie. It was research, and it had to be watched.

Ronald Elmtree was sprawled in his favourite armchair, with a leg hung over one of the chair's arms and a pile of insurance policies and clients' folders bundled on the other. Occasionally he would glance at the television and make a disapproving tut.

Eleanor and Oliver sat on the edge of the sofa. Greedy eyes watched the old black-and-white SF classic, *The Thing*. Eleanor knew the story but had never seen the film before. It was about a group of Arctic scientists who discover a flying saucer in the ice. They blow open the ice that has trapped the UFO and discover a frozen alien, probably the pilot of the saucer, in a block of ice. They bring the alien back to the base where, after a while, the ice melts and the alien is brought back to life. After many thrilling attempts to capture and destroy the creature, which they have identified as a threat to life on earth, they finally electrocute it.

Eleanor gasped at the final scene. One of the leading characters, with whom she had closely associated herself, glanced up at the skies.

"There are stranger things in heaven and earth," said the hero. "We must be aware. Watch the skies. Keep watching!"

"Did you hear?" said Eleanor. "Did you hear what he said? Keep watching, we must be aware!"

Mr Elmtree looked over one of his insurance forms.

"Utter nonsense!" he grunted, as he pointed the remote control at the screen and changed the channel to *Celebrity Guesses.*

Sidney the beagle shifted his bottom in disapproval. Eleanor gave one of her enormous sighs and pushed her spectacles up on to her nose.

"One must always be ready for the Unexplained, the Unknown!"

"Codswallop," mumbled Mr Elmtree.

"All right then," said Eleanor. "Can you tell me why people sometimes suddenly and mysteriously burst into flames?"

Oliver pinned back his ears and watched his older sister with a smile of admiration. It was going to be another one of 'those' discussions.

"People don't burst into flames," replied Mr Elmtree.

"They do so," said Eleanor. "It's well documented. All that's left is a sooty mark and ashes. It's called 'spontaneous combustion'. And where do these mysterious crop circles come from then?"

"Farmers having a laugh, messing around with tractors."

"Sometimes, maybe," conceded Eleanor. "But not always. And what about unexplained sightings of flying saucers, or UFOs as we Investigators of the Unexplained call them."

Sidney looked up and Oliver nodded.

"Weather balloons or strange-shaped aeroplanes."

"And what about objects that move about on their own? And people that can read other people's minds? What about ghosts? And how is it that Eric Froggat's grandfather knew who was going to win the Grand National Race this year?"

"Coincidence, imagination … "

"Then how come … ?"

"Eleanor!" shouted her father. "Enough is enough, for goodness sake."

"And where do all the lost socks go to?" asked Oliver quietly, who had been getting increasingly uncomfortable listening to Eleanor's list of all the world's great unsolved mysteries.

There was no answer to that one.

Ronald Elmtree swung his other leg over the arm of the chair and dropped his hands into his lap.

"This is all really getting out of hand, Eleanor. It's going to be time for bed soon, so get yourselves upstairs. Your mother will be home shortly."

Eleanor gave a big grin and kissed her father on the cheek. She felt quite certain that once again she had won the discussion. Those who are not Investigators of the Unexplained just do not understand.

"Dad," said Oliver quietly. "Can I leave my mobile downstairs, the one we made at school?"

"Sure. What's the problem then?"

Ronald Elmtree caught a nervous look in his son's eye.

"Nothing, no problem," Oliver replied curtly.

"We'll keep it in a drawer," said Eleanor.

"It's that darn film, isn't it?" said Mr Elmtree. "You ask if you can stay up to watch these monster movie things and then you get nervous about going to bed! I don't know."

Eleanor put her arm around her brother's shoulder.

"No, it's not that," she said defensively. "We've had other strange experiences lately. As Investigators, we need to be alert. We have reason to suspect that the mobile may have been made under the influence of an alien race. I think it's some kind of aerial or maybe a transmitter."

Sidney growled in agreement. Mr Elmtree looked completely perplexed.

CHAPTER 12

That night Oliver did not sleep soundly. He tossed and turned restlessly in his bed, imagining that he was being carried away within coloured orbs. Attempts to escape were hopeless. Oliver pressed his face into the soapy film that had become his prison, his mouth pushing against the yielding softness.

Awaking with a start, Oliver found that he had buried his head deeply into his pillow. His mouth was opening and closing like a landed fish, and the corner of his pillowcase felt like a wet rag.

From somewhere else within the darkness of the room he heard a low hiss, then a cackle, followed by the sound of the rasp of metal against metal like the sharpening of knives. Pulling the edge of his sheet up to his chin he stared into the darkness.

"Who's there?" he asked.

But there was no reply.

Instead, he once again heard the rasp of metal against metal. The cackle, like that of an old crone, disappeared into the mystery of the night. Oliver's imagination spiralled onward.

Somewhere outside, a wolf howled at the moon.

He heard the murmur of a night-shade as it passed through his wall, floating, pressing onward in its search for a final resting place.

"Such mysteries," said a voice beneath his bed.

Silver shards of moonlight passed through the bedroom windowpane throwing a flexing pattern, like the reflections of the scales of Martian Mogoloctic fire-fish as they leap up river to spawn.

The wolf howled once more.

Oliver felt the reality of the bed sheet and bit on the edge of his blanket.

"Wolf?" thought Oliver suddenly. "There aren't any wolves around here."

Elsewhere in the Elmtree household, Eleanor dreamt of space craft, of fleets of grotesquely-shaped ships, mixtures of geometric forms, which hovered at the edge of time. Waiting. Waiting.

Eleanor observed them from a distant place, helpless, unable to intervene. They were almost certainly an invasion fleet. Suddenly, one of the larger craft – a ship which appeared intertwined with another, making an enormous triangle – began to let out a blue glow. From within the triangular shapes, an enormous hatch started to lower itself. The blue glow became brighter and brighter as the door opened wider and wider.

Then, they came. In their hundreds at first, then in their thousands. Different shapes and sizes, colours and hues, but all with a metallic brightness which caught the light of the stars as they rotated, twisted and rolled like circus tumblers.

Coat hangers!

"No!" cried Eleanor. "No! Keep away!"

Many passed her by, some travelling at speed. Some had labels on them: one brown suit – to be ready by Thursday, children's slacks – collected Friday, corduroy jeans – reduced from £15. One pair had become enmeshed in wire – pierced as though by a dagger. Some had been bent into strange shapes: clips for radiator hoses, hooks to retrieve items, hangers for garden tools and pots of paint. Several had been bent into structures that would go round the U-bend in a sink.

Some were shaped into hoops.

Then, from within the blue light, Eleanor caught just a glimpse of a skeletal form. It walked on air, along the beam of blue light. Something kept obstructing her view. It was as though a giant wing repeatedly flapped in front of her.

A message whispered in her head.

"We come from a parallel world – we must not see ourselves!"

A howl rang out across the universe.

"Sidney!" cried Eleanor, as she sat upright. It was morning.

The bedroom door was ajar, held open by her brother Oliver. A very sorry-looking beagle plodded into the room. At first Eleanor wasn't sure what it was that he was wearing on his head: it looked as though it was a basket of some kind. Whatever it was, part of the structure was wound around his muzzle and strands of it reached around his ears. Sidney was very unhappy.

"I found him downstairs," said Oliver.

"What's that – that thing on his face?"

"I … er, … I think it's a coat hanger."

Sidney the beagle seemed to nod. He looked terribly sorry for himself.

All of a sudden their mother appeared in the hallway behind Oliver. She held a bundle of coat hangers and torn shreds of her best clothes in her arms.

"Has that dog been in our wardrobe?" she asked.

There was silence. Sidney, Oliver and Eleanor looked at each other. Virginia Elmtree noted the expressions.

"All right," she said. "Just what's going on here? And before we go any further take that ridiculous-looking thing off Sidney's face."

CHAPTER 13

Eleanor and Oliver sat quite, quite still, listening very carefully to the local radio station. They were listening to a new advertisement that appeared on Radio Kennet. The Otter twins had called Eleanor earlier, speaking from a pair of telephones simultaneously. They told her to listen for an advertisement from a company which called itself 'Dusk and Dawn'. Matthew had smelt a rat.

"Hi there, kids! Are you prepared for Stargate Night?" went the voice on the radio. "Because if you're not, then you'll be missing out in a big way! Free, with every dry cleaning contract this month, will be a special Galaxy Wand. The Dusk and Dawn Galaxy Wand will enable you to listen in to the conversations of the stars next Friday night, April the 30th, the night when the Asteroid from the end of the universe will pass by Earth on its million trillion mile journey through space!"

"I'd forgotten all about the asteroid!" said Oliver with raised eyebrows.

"Quiet!" snapped Eleanor. "I hadn't!"

"Just go out into your garden and raise the special Galaxy Wand into the air and through the aid of the special frequency you will hear the stars talk to one another! Hurry now – supplies are limited. Tell your mum and dad to get their cleaning at Dusk and Dawn this month!"

The message ended with a strange electronic tone which made Sidney the beagle raise one of his ears. The tone sounded like a far away radio signal, which twisted and played a peculiarly hypnotic jingle, almost like the sound of the quavering of a saw.

"The Otters were right – I smell a rat too. Who are Dusk and Dawn?"

Just then, their mother bounced into the kitchen.

"They are very good. It's this new chain of dry cleaners," said Mrs Elmtree, as she wrestled a clean blouse on to a suspiciously bright-coloured coat hanger.

"In fact," she continued, "I was just on my way there myself. Another shop has opened up in the High Street. Dorothy Otter and Mrs Johnson recommended it."

Eleanor and Oliver exchanged glances of insight.

From outside, in the garden, came the sound of Mr Elmtree cursing the garden gate.

"I damn well fixed this. Now it seems to have taken on a mind of its own!"

Oliver ran out to see what the problem was. Sidney got to their father ahead of him, but stopped abruptly in front of the gate. Sidney lowered his tail and growled.

"See, even Sidney thinks it's peculiar!" said Mr Elmtree.

"What is it?" asked Eleanor from the kitchen doorway.

"I'd mended this gate with a bit of wire. The latch wasn't working properly. Now look at it. It's almost as though the wire had taken on a life of its own and fastened the gate shut!"

Oliver and Eleanor approached the gate latch and inspected the repair.

"It's just like Mr Paddock-Smith's car," whispered Oliver.

A shining chrome wire had wrapped itself several times around the gatepost and then looped back on itself again into a knot.

"Look at it!" yelled Mr Elmtree again. "Nobody could have made anything like that, now could they?"

"I'm off to the cleaners!" called Mrs Elmtree from the side of the house. "Do you kids want to come with me? Thought you might be interested since there's some weird free gift going. You know how you like these space things."

Oliver and Eleanor nodded at one another.

Just as they turned to leave they caught sight of their father's face. His expression had changed to one of serious puzzlement. He was staring at one of the garden chairs which stood just outside the kitchen door.

Eleanor looked in the same direction as her father. The legs of the chair, usually a rusty-coloured metal, were gleaming – a bright chrome colour that seemed somehow to pulsate a special radiance beneath the warmth of the sun. Nearby lay the discarded remains of the coat hanger which Mr Elmtree had used to try to fix the garden gate.

It had started. Eleanor knew it.

CHAPTER 14

Mrs Elmtree parked their car in the supermarket car-park, just off the main road. Eleanor and Oliver's eyes were wide. Supermarket trolleys seemed to be everywhere, innocently pushed around by mothers and their little ones, children eager to assist. Assistants were busy returning them to the special compounds put aside for collection. Was the wire usually as bright as that? Had the supermarket trolleys always sparkled and radiated in that special way?

"Look at that," whispered Eleanor to Oliver.

Just ahead of them, a pair of trolleys were being pushed by two ladies in identical dresses, a summer blue colour. Both had children with them, a boy and a girl. For a moment the trolleys faced one another. One of the children raised a stick from which hung a bunch of silvery objects. The other child did the same, almost as if in salute. It might have been a trick of the light, but it seemed as though a spark danced across from one trolley to the other.

"Oh, my!" Eleanor sucked in her breath. "The mobiles!"

"Hey, did you see that?" asked Oliver.

Eleanor turned on her heels with a start.

"What? The lightning? Of course I did."

"No, no. Over there! It's gone now."

Oliver had pointed in the direction of the High Street.

"What was it?" asked Eleanor, her eyes scanning for any signs of alien activity.

"It was that chrome van again. It went round the back of one of the shops over there!"

"What are you kids on about now?" asked Mrs Elmtree as she slammed the boot of the car shut, and gathered up a bundle of clothes in her arms. "Come on, the place is over there, where those workmen are."

Together they walked out of the car-park, and into the turning which led to the High Street. Ahead of them a group of workmen were loading a large shop sign into the back of a pickup truck. The sign said 'ThoroClean'. Another group of workmen, who moved in a strangely angular manner like a collection of stick insects, were replacing the old sign with a new one. In bright shiny letters above the door of the dry cleaners was the name of the new company: Dusk and Dawn.

"There it is!" said Mrs Elmtree. "Come on, I've a lot to do today."

"The van, the one that I saw a moment ago, it went round the back of the shop," whispered Oliver.

"This is serious – I mean deadly serious," said Eleanor. "The invasion is more advanced than I thought."

Mrs Elmtree hurried towards the shop. Before her hand touched the handle a whirring noise sounded and the door opened for her. Eleanor and Oliver followed behind her. As soon as all three of them stepped inside, the door snapped shut like a Venus fly trap.

"Everything's shining!" hissed Eleanor.

Oliver simply gazed around him. All of the fittings were sleek and polished. There were chrome handles, chrome edging – even the window of the big drier at the rear of the shop had a wider band of chrome finish than was usual. Within the drum, a blue light glowed.

Eleanor nudged Oliver.

Behind the counter, with wide-mouthed grins like silvery crocodiles, were the two shop assistants. Both were almost identical – paste-mask faces and large brimmed hats which were pulled down so as to hide most of each face.

"A free gift," sighed the assistant on the left.

"You shall listen to the siren song of the stars on April the 30th," said the other, as he or she (it was impossible to tell which) reached out for one of the rods that were stacked in a bundle.

"Make sure that you point it to the north – a signal!"

"They're the same as we made at school," said Oliver.

But Eleanor was only half listening as her mother handed over the cleaning, folding it neatly on the counter. Eleanor was watching a scene through the open door at the back of the shop. A van in the rear yard had opened its doors. She gazed open-mouthed in horror as rows upon rows of shining metal hangers were unloaded. The driver wore a large familiar hat and for a moment she was sure it was a certain new supply teacher – the beard gave him away. The driver looked up, seemingly startled at finding that the back door had been left ajar. Then he saw Eleanor and froze.

"We've got to get out," cried Eleanor.

"What's wrong?" asked Mrs Elmtree, suddenly glancing down at her daughter.

"No time to explain," said Eleanor.

The two assistants stared at one another in a manner as perfectly symmetrical as the Otters. One swiftly removed the clothes from the counter and handed Mrs Elmtree a ticket.

"Children!" exclaimed the assistant who was standing on the right. "Such imaginations, all of them! Come back later for the cleaning. Two new wands will be yours."

"And a pair of our special hangers," said the other with a smile.

Mrs Elmtree glanced at her ticket.

"Oh," she said, "I see that your main warehouse is in the new industrial estate? Unit 9, eh? That's near where we live. I've been trying to arrange an appointment to see your manager. Could I interest you in some insurance?"

"Insurance?" asked one of the assistants. "What is that?"

CHAPTER 15

Mr and Mrs Elmtree were out for the evening, completely unaware of the problems of the survival of the human race with which their children were left to wrestle. Eleanor curled her legs underneath her and kept watching the TV screen. Every so often her fingers lifted to her lips, a nervous gesture she sometimes displayed when deeply concerned. Tonight, Eleanor Elmtree was *very* deeply concerned.

Oliver watched his sister from the other chair. Sidney the beagle watched both of them from over the edge of his paws. The Saturday Evening TV Classic was just finishing. It was a science fiction film, another old black-and-white classic: *The Invasion of the Body Snatchers.* The film told the story of how aliens from outer space were able to take over the bodies of earth people. Very gradually, unnoticeably at first, the earth was invaded by a race of vegetable people. Nobody believed the main character, the hero who saw and was aware. Eleanor strongly felt in sympathy with the hero, who had to flee from town at the end.

"Do you see?" said Eleanor. "See how easy it is, how they can creep up on you, without you knowing."

Oliver nodded and said nothing. This time he knew it was for real. Something was happening in Dale Heath.

"We are being invaded, taken over in just the same way that it happened in the film. Not vegetable people, though –

coat hangers! An alien race of coat hangers, perhaps from another universe, or even from a parallel universe. Who knows?"

Oliver nodded again. Sidney made a small whining sound.

"Everyone uses coat hangers. They enter our lives unnoticed. We hang our clothes on them but we use them for other things too: cleaning drains, fixing gates and water hoses, retrieving things from difficult places. And at school … "

She paused to take a deep breath.

"And at school, we stupidly make mobiles. Quickly, let me see if there is any change."

Oliver solemnly rose out of his chair and crossed the room to the sideboard. He opened the drawer and took out a bundle wrapped in a polythene bag. Carefully he unwrapped the polythene and took out his mobile. In the half light of the sitting room, the silvery objects which hung from the end of the stick appeared to glitter and shine with a soft blue light. They had been carefully monitoring the mobile ever since their suspicions had been aroused.

"See," said Eleanor. "Look and be aware."

Together they stared at the mobile with intense eyes.

"There is change," said Eleanor in a low voice.

Oliver wasn't so certain, but he trusted his sister's judgement without question.

"It is beginning to signal; the blue light tells us that. Whatever happens, we must keep it for evidence or we'll never be believed later. Put it back in the drawer, we must not allow it to send messages."

Oliver placed the mobile back into the drawer. Suddenly a strange electronic tone almost made the fruit bowl on the table shudder.

Eleanor and Oliver twisted sharply round and glared at the TV set. The advertisement was on again. The message 'Dusk and Dawn Dry Cleaners – the cleaners you can rely on' glowed out from the screen.

A syrupy voice filled the sitting room. "Hey you kids, tomorrow night is the night of the Dusk and Dawn Galaxy Wands. Be sure to be out in your gardens with your special Dusk and Dawn wands. Point them at the stars. Point them, and be amazed!"

Eleanor shot across the room and picked up a copy of her father's newspaper. She looked at the date: Saturday 29th April.

"Tomorrow's the 30th!" she cried.

Oliver nodded. "Yes, of course. But what's the matter?"

Eleanor narrowed her eyes.

"Get on the phone to the Otters. We need an emergency meeting. It's the night of the asteroid, isn't it?"

Oliver's jaw slackened.

"But Patrick Morris is wrong, it's not an asteroid at all," continued Eleanor, lifting her fingers to her lips again. "Suddenly everything makes sense, everything comes together. The mother ship lands tomorrow. Tomorrow is the night of the invasion. Every stupid kid that goes into his or her back garden with a mobile, or a wand or whatever you call it, is sending a landing signal to the alien craft! Dale Heath is set up to become a huge airstrip and they are getting us to provide it."

Oliver's face dissolved into a mask of utter horror.

"The Otter twins, quickly," cried Eleanor. "We need the full team of the Investigators of the Unexplained. We must be ready for tomorrow night!"

Oliver Elmtree had already dialled the number.

CHAPTER 16

With steel-eyed determination in their faces, the Investigators of the Unexplained strode forward, in the direction of the industrial units area. As they passed through the Dale Heath housing estate they noticed how everything had started to change. Children's faces seemed to be watching them from every window, eager hands held the strange wands with the glowing silvery shapes at the end. Beneath a solitary streetlamp a supermarket trolley had been abandoned. The wire carriage seemed to glow with a sinister blue sheen. Simon noticed a discarded coat hanger lying in the gutter. It appeared to pulsate, to throb as though it had a life of its own. In some of the gardens, children had already started to appear with the wands from Dusk and Dawn. Many were pointing their sticks eagerly into the air with an enthusiasm that caused Eleanor to shudder. They could not be sure, but tonight the night sky appeared to fold over them like a huge cobalt cloak – as though a night dame, a mistress of darkness, had passed by.

Finally, they turned the corner and stood at the top of the road that led down to unit number 9.

"Remember to stick to the plan," said Eleanor.

"Simon and me round the back of the unit," said Matthew.

"And Oliver and you round the front," said Simon.

"Right," said Eleanor.

"But what can we actually do?" asked Oliver sensibly.

That point was still uncertain. Eleanor gritted her teeth, irritated by the detail.

"Observe, be aware. And, if necessary, sabotage. That's what we must do – sabotage their scheme! In theory there shouldn't be anybody there on a Sunday. But those are the rules for a regular organisation, NOT an alien one. They'll be there all right. It's the night!"

The Otters sniffed in agreement.

The Otter twins had crept around the side of unit number 9. Eleanor and Oliver crouched in the doorway of a neighbouring unit, watching and waiting. They were to wait for ten minutes and then make their way inside. The place was a hive of activity, as Eleanor had predicted. The chrome van was parked at the front. Stick-like people continued to step through the small door in the front shutters of the unit. Their faces all showed the same expression – a neutral blank gaze, eyeless and somehow far-seeing. They would gaze up at the stars, nod and return inside.

"They all look like our teacher," said Oliver.

"And ours," said Eleanor, "though of course, you must remember that Mr Kite and Miss Moonfleet are not our teachers. They are aliens."

Oliver stood up.

"Could … could it be that we are mistaken? I mean, are we certain that they are aliens?"

"Nothing is certain," replied Eleanor. "In this life, who knows anything for sure?"

Oliver nodded. This seemed reasonable.

Suddenly the night sky lit up, a brilliant spangle-shaped star burst, like a firework spread above them. Oliver glanced upwards.

"The asteroid!" he screamed.

"No! Not any asteroid. Look!"

They both stared as the lights in the sky seemed to hover above them for a matter of seconds before moving into a form, a certain geometrical shape. The pulses of fire, like

Guy Fawkes rockets, shot lines of light to one another. Within moments, above them in the cobalt-coloured darkness, a pair of interlocking triangles were formed. In the centre, where they overlapped, a shimmering vortex of silver light began to whirl. Something twisted and turned within the shape, something from a darker place.

"It's a star gate. I know it is," said Eleanor.

In the distance they watched as tiny spots of light from the gardens of Dale Heath houses suddenly popped alight like glow worms. The airstrip for the craft was being completed.

"We've no time to lose," said Eleanor. "Mankind and the survival of our planet are at risk!"

Eleanor noticed that the door of the unit was open. One of the figures had just passed through it to inspect the sky. It was standing in front of the van, shielding its eyes and watching the night sky intently.

"Let's go. Be aware!" cried Eleanor.

Eleanor and Oliver rushed out from their cover.

A shaft of light spilled out through the doorway. Without a second's thought they rushed in through the door – and stopped dead in their tracks the moment they saw what they saw.

"Damn it. As I suspected! This is no dry cleaners," said Eleanor.

Oliver stood with his mouth open.

The inside of the unit was like a massive gleaming furnace of shimmering silver. Everywhere were rows and rows of garment rails from which hung hundreds and thousands of coat hangers, all interlocking into spectacular shapes as they swung freely from the rail.

Wire-framed figures, like skeletal robots, worked ceaselessly to hang more and more hangers on the rails. Some of the figures made no attempt to hide the fact that they were alien creatures. Some wore clothes which flapped and wrapped around their wiry limbs. There were no faces, simply something soft and rubbery which was shaped into some form of human face. They all looked like Mr Kite and Miss Moonfleet.

Eleanor was transfixed, unable to move from the spot where she stood. But Oliver noticed. At the far end of the unit there was a central platform, like a suspended floor. In the centre was an enormous silver archway formed from two triangles. The top of the triangle stretched up to the roof, which opened to the night sky. From it shot a bolt of light – just the same as the lightning bolt they had seen before – up into the heavens.

"It's making contact with the mother ship!" said Oliver.

Eleanor nodded furiously. Something else held her attention. To the right of the triangle, in a soapy bubble structure, were the Otter twins. Their terrified faces were pushed against the surface of the skin of the bubble. Opposite, on the other side of the star gate, was another bubble, and in this one were two more very sorry-looking human figures.

"They've got the Otters! And it's Mr Polkinghorne!" cried Eleanor.

"And Miss Perkins, our teacher!" said Oliver.

From out of nowhere a massive pair of wiry claws descended, and held both of them by the arms. It was Mr

Kite. This time his voice sound metallic and boomy, like the resounding echo in a cave.

"Too bad. Such wonders, eh? You cannot stop us now. In just a few more minutes we will have enough radiated power from Dale Heath, thanks to its enthusiastic children, for the corridor from your universe to ours to be complete. We will enter, all of us, and take over the dry cleaning centres of the world! Our mirror universe will be one with yours!"

Eleanor turned her face towards her captor.

"Mirror?"

"Yes, we are your opposite, from another dimension in space and time. We have come to claim."

"Parallel world!" yelled Oliver. "Like we read about in the magazine!"

Eleanor looked ahead of her. Something was coming through the corridor, from the star gate in the sky. A sudden ultrabright shaft of light throbbed between the forms of the Otters and the teachers. Within the light something twisted and turned like a molten ball of slippery, slimy quicksilver string. The wire ones would be here very soon.

"You are powerless!" called a voice from their left. It was Miss Moonfleet. "Our people are coming!"

"Not if I can help it!" cried Eleanor.

With that, she dropped down and ducked under Mr Kite's arm.

"She can do nothing!" said Miss Moonfleet.

But Eleanor was aware. Eleanor Elmtree knew the laws of astrophysics, of positive and negative and the laws of mirrors.

"Opposites cancel each other out!" she cried to Oliver.

Eleanor was free. She rushed to the control panel at the side of the massive roller shutter door and, with gritted teeth, she threw the switch.

The unit was filled with the hum of a hydraulic engine, as slowly the shutters rose.

"That'll do you no good!" cried Mr Kite as he let go of Oliver.

"We'll see," snarled Eleanor.

The shutters rose, higher and higher.

All of a sudden a scream, piercing and shrill, cut through the air.

"The earth vehicle!" cried Miss Moonfleet. "It's outside the doors!"

"So wha … ?"

Mr Kite never completed his sentence.

The silvery furnace, through which the invading army was about to emerge, suddenly shook. A bolt of blue spat from its centre and bounced off the mirror reflection of the scene which now shimmered in the side of the chrome van.

"A mirror!" cried Oliver with delight. "Eleanor, you're a genius!"

"Let them cancel each other out!" cried Eleanor Elmtree. "Negative and positive equals … "

"Nothing!" danced Oliver.

"This isn't the art room mirror this time, Mr Kite! It's made of your own metal!"

Mr Kite's face began to dissolve from off the wire frame. From somewhere within the very heart of the building an anguished voice shook and raged.

"Aaaagggh! Damn you, earthlings! You have won this time! But only this time ... We shall return!"

"May you rust in hell!" screamed Eleanor.

In a flash of blue the wire ones vanished, leaving only the Investigators of the Unexplained, the two school teachers and somebody's uncollected brown corduroy trousers, left there since Monday.

EPILOGUE

When Eleanor and Oliver arrived home they discovered that Aunt Eloise, from South Carolina, USA, had already arrived. Eleanor burst in through the front door, and was the first to see the huge bags in the hallway.

"It's Aunt Eloise," said Oliver without too much enthusiasm.

Eleanor lifted her finger to her lips.

"We must search her luggage," she said. "You know our rules."

"You'll do nothing of the kind!" said Mrs Elmtree, who was in the kitchen preparing tea, and who had heard Eleanor's comment. "This thing of yours is getting out of hand!"

"But we have to be sure," insisted Eleanor.

"Stuff and stupidity," said Mrs Elmtree. "This wire thing nonsense is … well, it's just nonsense!"

Mrs Elmtree swept past the two children with a tray. From the sitting room came the sing-song tone of Aunt Eloise's voice.

"Nobody believes us," moaned Oliver.

And it was true, nobody did. Patrick Morris on the TV had claimed that the dramatic display in the sky on the night of April the 30th had been due to a passing asteroid, as he had predicted. Mr Polkinghorne and Miss Perkins had both suffered a complete loss of memory due to Eleanor's reversal of the star gate. They could remember nothing since the start of the school term, putting the explanation down to a common virus. Of course, there were mysteries which were inexplicable: why a new chain of dry cleaners should suddenly vanish, for instance. But certainly nothing paranormal.

Only the Investigators of the Unexplained knew. Only the Investigators of the Unexplained were aware.

"We have a national duty," said Eleanor. "We must check everything. Under no circumstances must wire coat hangers enter this house."

Eleanor knelt down and began to unclip the huge belt that circled one of Aunt Eloise's cases. The case itself was unlocked. First there was a set of towels, then several skirts, then something soft and slippery like polythene.

"Newly-cleaned clothes," whispered Eleanor.

Oliver slid his hand beneath the bundle and helped Eleanor lift them out of the case.

Suddenly the voices in the sitting room rose. Before either Oliver or Eleanor could put the clothes back, Aunt Eloise stood in the doorway.

"Eleanor!" screamed their mother, who hovered anxiously behind their aunt. "I told you!"

"Oh, it's nothing," sang Aunt Eloise. "The dahhlings are jus' helpin' their Aunty unpack, aren't y'all, sweeties?"

Eleanor gulped.

In the doorway, Sidney the beagle growled.

"Mind how you go now though. Jus' had that lot cleaned at a brand spanking new chain of cleaners that's opened up all over the States. Catchy name too: Dusk and Dawn.

Snakes alive, the President of the United States himself has his dry cleaning done there too!"

Oliver Elmtree trembled as his sister carefully withdrew a shining silver hanger from out of one of their aunt's dresses.

"Be aware," declared Eleanor Elmtree. "They're back."

Oliver reached for the hall phone to call the Otters.